December 25 1992
Merry With love—
John, Aunts Diane,
Christi + Emilie

RAIN

DROP

SPLASH

STORY BY ALVIN TRESSELT

PICTURES BY LEONARD WEISGARD

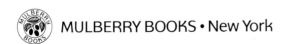

MULBERRY BOOKS • New York

Drip drop splash,
drip drop splash,
drip drop splash
went the rain all day.

Dripped from the
shiny leaves,
dropped from a
rabbit's nose,
splashed from
a brown
bear's tail.

Fell from a daisy's face, trickled down the tree trunks, and splunked on a green frog's back.

There were so many rain drops
they made a puddle.
The puddle grew larger, and
larger, and larger, until it
became a pond. Water-lilies
floated on it, little fish
swam in it, and tiny snails
sat beside it.

Still it rained. Drip
drop splash, drip drop splash,
drip drop splash.
The little pond grew larger and
larger and spilled right over
into a brook.

Tumbling
and splashing
and running down
the mountain. Scared
a chipmunk, splashed
some violets, passed a
mother deer showing her
baby how to drink.

Jumped over big stones, fell into deep pools, and rested on a bed of soft green moss. Then tumbled into a lake.

Now it was a big lake, with big fish and tall pickerel weed. Dragonflies skimmed over

the water, turtles floated quietly, and a red
winged blackbird built his nest in the rushes.

Still it rained. Drip drop splash,
drip drop splash, drip drop splash.
The lake grew larger and larger.
It flooded a farmer's meadow
and the cows stood in the mud.

It covered a road
and the cars couldn't pass
and the children
had to go to school in a boat.

Then it overflowed into a river, with houses and towns along the shore. It ran under bridges and

over waterfalls. Men fished from the rocks, and two teams had a boat race.

Past factories and warehouses, the river came to great cities with docks. There were ships and barges

and scows and tankers, and a
boatful of people
on a holiday.

Little boys jumped into the water,
subway trains and cars
ran under it, ferry boats puffed
back and forth on top,
and seagulls flew over it
looking for fish to eat.

Then it passed a fort
and a lighthouse and a bell buoy,
and the river flowed into the sea.

Tall waves rolled up
to meet it.
There was an ocean liner
with lots of little tug boats
guiding it. The sun came out,
and at last the rain stopped.

Afterword

RAIN DROP SPLASH started out as a mountain stream named Hyacinth, and I was going to follow her down the mountain until she eventually reached the sea. But somewhere along the journey my personified brook got hopelessly lost, and I realized that this approach would never work. I then decided to "tell it like it is," and I traced the rain falling on a mountainside and making its way to the sea in a completely realistic manner. I accomplished this in less than five hundred words. The story was accepted, and Leonard Weisgard was asked to illustrate it. As a result, my very first book for children was named a Caldecott Medal Honor Book in 1947. and from it countless children have been learning about the natural progression of rainfall from brook to lake to river to the sea ever since.

Copyright © 1946 by Lothrop, Lee and Shepard Company
Copyright © 1990 by Alvin Tresselt

All rights reserved. No part of this book may be
reproduced or utilized in any form or by any means,
electronic or mechanical, including photocopying,
recording, or by any information storage or retrieval
system, without permission in writing from the Publisher.
Inquiries should be addressed to Lothrop, Lee and Shepard Books,
a division of William Morrow & Company, Inc.,
105 Madison Avenue, New York, New York 10016.

Library of Congress Cataloging in Publication Data

Tresselt, Alvin R. Rain drop splash / story by Alvin Tresselt ,
pictures by Leonard Weisgard. p. cm.
Summary· Follows the rain as it travels through a pond, a brook,
a lake, and a river down to the sea.
[1 Rain and rainfall—Fiction.] I. Weisgard, Leonard, 1916– ill.
II. Title. PZ7 T732Rai 1990 [E]—dc20 46-11878 CIP AC
ISBN 0-688-09352-3

Printed in Singapore
First Mulberry Edition, 1990
1 3 5 7 9 10 8 6 4 2